Night & Day

BOOK ONE
Reading for the Adult Learner of ESL/EFL

Caroline Banks

Maryann Orlando

Regents / Prentice Hall
Englewood Cliffs, New Jersey

Editorial/Production Supervision
   and Interior Design: *Ros Herion Freese*
Acquisitions Editor: *Nancy Leonhardt*
Cover Design: *Bert Adler/Superstock*
Illustrator: *Nicholas Read*
Prepress Buyer and Scheduler: *Ray Keating*
Manufacturing Buyer: *Lori Bulwin*

 © 1994 by Regents/Prentice Hall, Prentice-Hall, Inc.
A Paramount Communications Company
Englewood Cliffs, New Jersey 07632

All rights reserved. No part of this book may be
reproduced, in any form or by any means,
without permission in writing from the publisher.

Printed in the United States of America

10 9 8 7 6 5 4 3 2 1

ISBN   0-13-043696-8

Prentice-Hall International (UK) Limited, *London*
Prentice-Hall of Australia Pty. Limited, *Sydney*
Prentice-Hall Canada, Inc., *Toronto*
Prentice-Hall Hispanoamerica, S.A., *Mexico*
Prentice-Hall of India Private Limited, *New Delhi*
Prentice-Hall of Japan, Inc., *Tokyo*
Simon & Schuster Asia Pte. Ltd., *Singapore*
Editora Prentice-Hall do Brasil, Ltda., *Rio de Janeiro*

Contents

About the Authors   iv
To the Teacher   v
To the Student   vi
Introduction   vii

PART ONE: Who are we?   1

   1. Who are you?   3
   2. What's this book about?   11
   3. Where, oh where?   19
   4. Say when ...   27
   5. Why? ... Why not?   35

PART TWO: From Today to Tomorrow   43

   6. What is good to eat?   45
   7. How are you feeling?   53
   8. It's an emergency!   61
   9. There's no place like home ...   69
  10. Help Wanted   77

PART THREE: How do you like it here?   85

  11. Take me out to the ball game ...   87
  12. Too Many, Too Much   95
  13. Loss   103
  14. Love   111
  15. Life   119

LEARNING GUIDE   127

Target Words, Answers to Word Checkout, Suggestions for Students, The English Alphabet, Days of the Week, Months and Seasons of the Year, Colors, Numbers, Languages of the World (other than English)

About the Authors

Caroline Banks teaches at Arlington High School, in Arlington, Massachusetts. She is also the author of several ESL textbooks, including *Readings in English*.

Maryann Orlando teaches Drama at Arlington High School and also teaches adult ESL.

They are both interested in family literacy.

To the Teacher

This book is for adult students who know how to read a little English. It may be helpful for your students to review the alphabet, numbers, days, month, and colors before starting the first lesson. You will find a review section in the Learning Guide at the end of this book.

The purpose of *Night & Day* is to give adult students a chance to read about and discuss many topics of daily interest, and to expand their knowledge of American culture.

Our approach will work well in a classroom atmosphere that encourages participation and cooperation. We have integrated all readings with active discussion.

Organization of Contents

Part One is organized around the "5Ws," the question words *who*, *what*, *where*, *when*, and *why*.

Part Two presents the topics of good nutrition, health, housing, and jobs.

Part Three presents the topics of sports, shopping, and cultural concerns about the issues of funerals, love, and birth.

Many more suggestions for teaching the material in this book can be found in the Teacher's Guide that accompanies all three levels of *Night & Day*.

To the Student

  We wrote this book for you. We hope you enjoy it. Take a look at the Contents. This book contains lessons about many topics.
  At the end of the book you will find the Learning Guide. We have listed the new words from each lesson. You will also find the answers to "Word Checkout."
  Happy reading!

Introduction

WORDS TO USE IN CLASS

Please turn to page 10.

Please look at Lesson 1.

Please read the directions.

Please talk about the picture.

Please talk about Reading 1.

Please talk about yourself.

Please write about it.

Please listen to the question.

Please say the answer.

Please fill in the spaces below.

Please talk with family and friends.

THE LESSONS
Please look at Lesson 1. Read the directions. All the lessons are like Lesson 1.

Pictures: Please talk about the picture.

READING 1:	Please talk about Reading 1.
Please talk about yourself.

THE WORD BASKET:	1. Find the new words.
2. Say the new words.
3. Write the new words.
4. Understand the new words.
5. Study the new words.

READING 2:	Please talk about Reading 2.
Please write about yourself.
Please talk to family and friends.

THE WORD STORE:	Information about words.

WORD CHECKOUT

WORDS "TO GO"

THE CARD SHOP

viii

PART ONE

Who are we?

PART ONE of this book is about you. You will ask many, many questions—and answer them. You will read and talk about:

>how to use this book,
>
>who is in the class,
>
>what your book is about,
>
>where you come from,
>
>where you live,
>
>when you do things every day,
>
>and
>
>why you are here.

LESSON 1

Who are you?

Please talk about the picture.

1. Tell about the people in the picture.

2. Why are they there?

READING 1

Who am I? Who are you?

Who am I?

>Am I my name?

>Am I my face?

>Am I my voice and my words?

>Am I my body?

Who are you?

>Are you your family?

>Are you your work?

>Are you your past and your dreams?

>Are you your country?

>Are you you? or we?

I am. You are. We are.

And more.

Please talk about Reading 1.

1. What "big" questions does the writer ask?

2. What does this mean: "Are you your past and your dreams?"

3. What does this mean: "Are you you? or we?"

4. The writer says: "And more." What does this mean?

Please talk about yourself.

1. Please introduce yourself to the class. Tell your name.

2. What is your work?

3. Who is in your family?

4. What are your dreams?

THE WORD BASKET

Here is a way to learn new words. Use these five steps.

STEP 1: Go back to Reading 1. Read it again. Find the words you want to remember. Write them in the spaces below:

New Words

1. _____
2. _____
3. _____
4. _____
5. _____
6. _____
7. _____
8. _____
9. _____
10. _____

STEP 2: Say your new words to the class. Your classmates will say their new words. Do you want to add other new words? Do it here:

Other New Words

_____

_____

STEP 3: Work with the class. Find out the meanings of your words. Write the new words and their meanings in English (or in your language) in the spaces below:

New Words   **Meanings**

1. _____   _____

2. _____   _____

3. _____   _____

4. _____   _____

5. _____   _____

6. _____   _____

7. _____   _____

8. _____   _____

9. _____   _____

10. _____   _____

Other New Words

_____   _____

_____   _____

STEP 4: Go back to Reading 1. Read it again. Now look at the list of **Target Words** for this lesson on page 127 of the Learning Guide. Do you want to change your list? Do that now.

STEP 5: Use your lists to help you remember your new words. Use these same five steps for Reading 2.

READING 2

I Am More

Who am I?

    Look at my face. Look at my body.

    Listen to my voice. Listen to my words.

    And listen to my name.

    They are all important.

But I am more.

    I am my past.

    I am my family, and my family is me.

    I am my country.

    I am my dreams.

Please talk about Reading 2.

1. The writer says: "Look at _____ . Look at _____ ."

2. The writer says: "Listen to _____ . Listen to _____ . And listen to _____ ."

3. The writer says: "I am more." What does this mean?

4. The writer says: "I am my dreams." What does this mean?

Please write about it.
Find some sentences you like from Reading 2. Write them here:

1. _____
2. _____
3. _____
4. _____

Please talk with family and friends.
Ask these questions. Ask two or three people. Tell the class the answers next time.
1. Do you like your name? Why? Why not?
2. Which is more important to you—your family or your work? Why?

THE WORD STORE

Question Word: *Who?*
Who am I?
Who are you?

Subject Pronouns with *to be*

I am.	Am I?	Who am I?
You are.	Are you?	Who are you?
It is.	Is it?	Who is it?
She is.	Is she?	Who is she?
He is.	Is he?	Who is he?
We are.	Are we?	Who are we?
They are.	Are they?	Who are they?

Sentence Pattern: Subject/Linking Verb/Adjective

I	am	important.	
My past	is	important.	It is important.
My friend	is	important.	He is important. She is important.
My dreams	are	important.	They are important.
You	are	important.	
We	are	important.	

9

WORD CHECKOUT

Please check yourself.
Put a check (4) next to each sentence that is true about you.

____ My body is important.

____ My name is important.

____ My family is important.

____ My work is important.

____ My country is important.

____ My language is important.

____ My voice is important.

____ My past is important.

____ My dreams are important.

WORDS "TO GO"

> We are the world.
> I think, therefore I am.

THE CARD SHOP

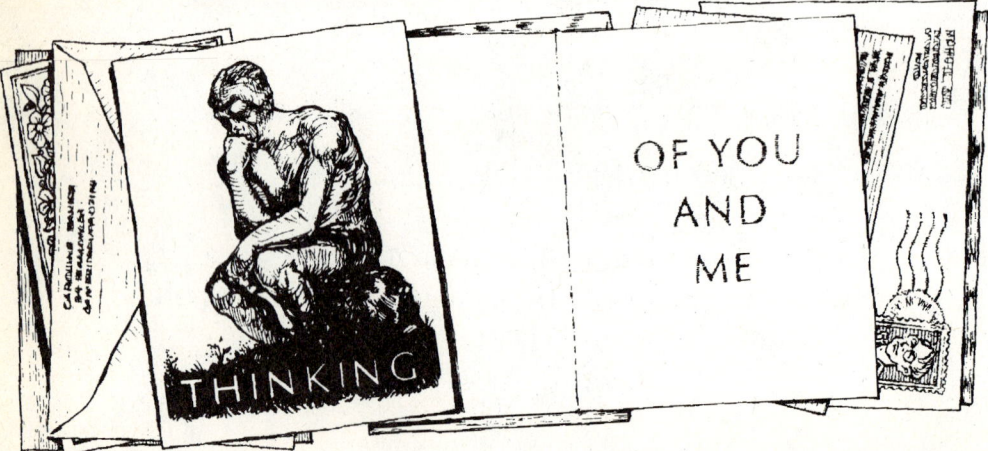

LESSON 2
What's this book about?

Please look at the cover of your book.
Talk about it.
  1. What's the title?
  2. What's the book about?

Please look at the Contents of your book on page iii.
Talk about the lessons.

READING 1

What's the answer?

Questions	Answers
What's your first name?	Amalia.
What's your last name, your family name?	Smith.
What's your address?	3102 Main Street.
What's your first language?	English.
What's your telephone number?	(617) 555–4706.

Please talk about Reading 1.

1. Is Amalia a man or a woman?

2. Is "Amalia" a first or a last name?

3. Is "Smith" a family name or a first name?

4. What is the number of the house on Main Street where Amalia Smith lives?

5. What language did Amalia Smith learn first?

6. Talk about telephone numbers.

Please talk about yourself.

1. Please tell the class your full name: your first name and your last name.

2. Is your family name your first name or your last name?

3. Talk about the names in your class. Talk about first names and last names.

4. Tell the class your first language. (Look on page 136 in the Learning Guide for a list of languages other than English.)

THE WORD BASKET

Here is a way to learn new words. Use these five steps.

STEP 1: Go back to Reading 1. Read it again. Find the words you want to remember. Write them in the spaces below:

New Words

1. _____
2. _____
3. _____
4. _____
5. _____
6. _____
7. _____
8. _____
9. _____
10. _____

STEP 2: Say your new words to the class. Your classmates will say their new words. Do you want to add other new words? Do it here:

Other New Words

_____

_____

STEP 3: Work with the class. Find out the meanings of your words. Write the new words and their meanings in English (or in your language) in the spaces below:

New Words   **Meanings**

1. _____   _____
2. _____   _____
3. _____   _____
4. _____   _____
5. _____   _____
6. _____   _____
7. _____   _____
8. _____   _____
9. _____   _____
10. _____   _____

Other New Words

_____   _____

_____   _____

STEP 4: Go back to Reading 1. Read it again. Now look at the list of **Target Words** for this lesson on page 128 of the Learning Guide. Do you want to change your list? Do that now.

STEP 5: Use your lists to help you remember your new words. Use these same five steps for Reading 2.

READING 2

Am I the only student?

It's the first night of the class. Carlos enters the classroom. He's early. He sits down and looks at the room. He's alone. He feels a little nervous.

I'm the first student here.

What's this? The book!

Hmmm…. A picture on the cover. OK.

The title is *Night & Day*. OK.

It's about night and day?

What!? Reading all night and all day?

What's on page iii? The Contents. 15 Lessons.

Hmmm…. 136 pages.

Look! A list of languages is on page 136.

What about the alphabet? Oh. OK. Hmmm….

Other students enter the classroom. The teacher enters. The class begins.

Please talk about Reading 2.

1. Who is Carlos?
2. What does Carlos do in the classroom?
3. How does Carlos feel?
4. What is on page 136 of the book?
5. What is on page 135?

Please write about it.
Write about your book. Fill in the spaces below:

Title: _____

Number of pages: _____

Number of lessons: _____

What's it about? _____

Please talk with family and friends.
Ask two friends to write their names. Talk to them about first names and family names. Write the names. Talk about the names in class next time.

THE WORD STORE

Question Word: *What?*
what's = what is
What's the answer?
What's your name?
What's your address?

Possessive Adjectives
my	my book	my name	my address
your	your book	your name	your address
its	its book	its name	its address
her	her book	her name	her address
his	his book	his name	his address
our	our book	our name	our address
their	their book	their name	their address

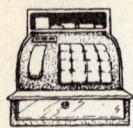

WORD CHECKOUT

Please check yourself.
Write about yourself. Fill in the spaces below:

First name:_____

Last name: _____

Address: _____

Telephone number:_____

First language: _____

Fill in the spaces below. Use *your* or *my*.

1. What's your first name? _____ first name is Carlos.
2. What's _____ last name? My last name is Costa.
3. What's your first language? _____ first language is Spanish.

WORDS "TO GO"

What's it all about?
What's new?

THE CARD SHOP

LESSON 3
Where, oh where?

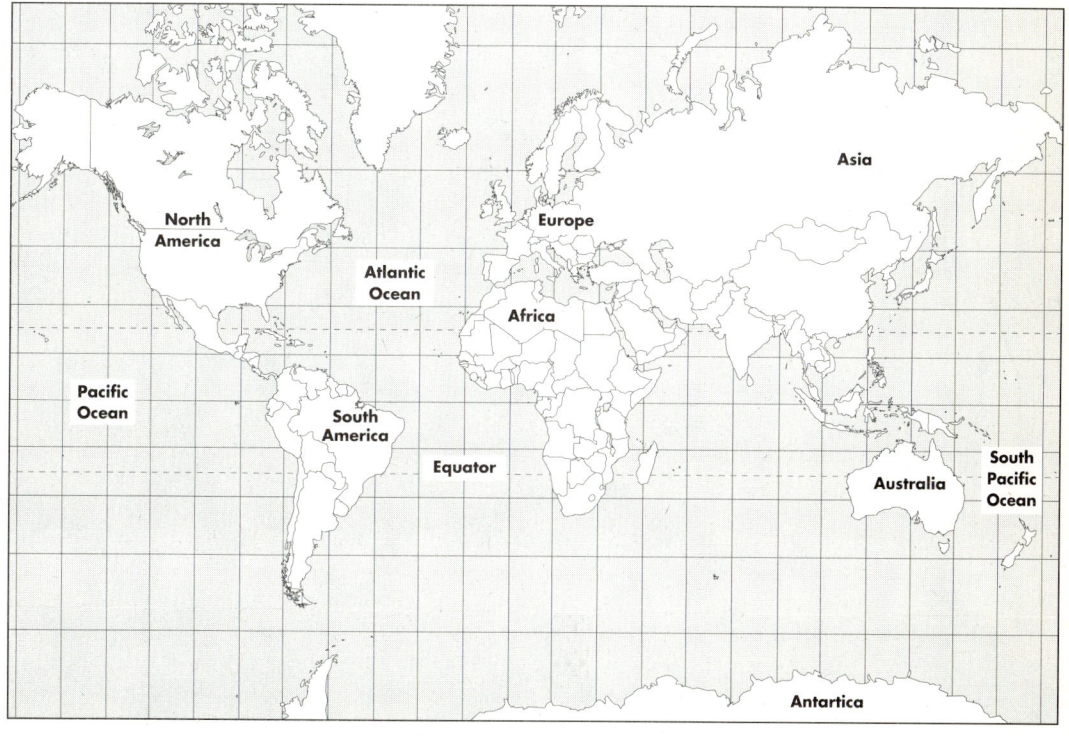

Please talk about the map.
1. Find the places you know on the map.
2. Find the country you are from.
3. Tell about the country you are from.
4. What other countries do you know about?

READING 1

Where, oh where?

Where do you live?

In a house or a car?

In a room or a tent?

In a trailer?

In a hotel?

Do you live in an apartment?

In a condo?

In a castle?

Do you live on a boat?

In your coat?

Where, oh where?

Please talk about Reading 1.

   1. Talk about the new words.

   2. Are a condo and an apartment the same or different?

   3. What does this mean: "Do you live…in your coat?"

   4. Who lives in a castle?

Please talk about yourself.

   1. Where do you live now?

   2. Where did you live before?

   3. Tell about your dream house.

THE WORD BASKET

Here is a way to learn new words. Use these five steps.

STEP 1: Go back to Reading 1. Read it again. Find the words you want to remember. Write them in the spaces below:

New Words

1. _____
2. _____
3. _____
4. _____
5. _____
6. _____
7. _____
8. _____
9. _____
10. _____

STEP 2: Say your new words to the class. Your classmates will say their new words. Do you want to add other new words? Do it here:

Other New Words

_____

_____

STEP 3: Work with the class. Find out the meanings of your words. Write the new words and their meanings in English (or in your language) in the spaces below:

New Words   **Meanings**

1. _____   _____

2. _____   _____

3. _____   _____

4. _____   _____

5. _____   _____

6. _____   _____

7. _____   _____

8. _____   _____

9. _____   _____

10. _____   _____

Other New Words

_____   _____

_____   _____

STEP 4: Go back to Reading 1. Read it again. Now look at the list of **Target Words** for this lesson on page 128 of the Learning Guide. Do you want to change your list? Do that now.

STEP 5: Use your lists to help you remember your new words. Use these same five steps for Reading 2.

READING 2

Home

Where am I from? I'm from a different country. That was home. I lived in a house before. That was home.

Now I live in a new country. I live in an apartment. Now I have two homes.

Before, we lived in a small house. It was a lovely house. We were happy.

Now we live in a small apartment. It's a modern apartment. It's small, but it's comfortable.

Is a house the same as home? A house or an apartment is a place to sleep and eat. But home is more. Home is a place, a very important place. Where is home for me? Home is where my heart is.

Please talk about Reading 2.

1. Where did the writer live before?

2. Where does the writer live now?

3. Tell about the writer's apartment.

4. The writer says: "Home is where my heart is." What does this mean?

Please write about it.

1. Where are you from?
2. Where did you live before?
3 Where do you live now?
4. Do you like your home? Why? Why not?
5. Where is home for you? Why?

Please talk with family and friends.
Ask your friends about home. Ask them these questions: Where do you live? Do you like it? Did you live in a different country before? Where? Tell the class the answers next time.

THE WORD STORE

Question Word: *Where?*
Where are you from?
Where do you live?
Where is your home?

Simple Present of *to live*

Where do you live now?	I live in an apartment.
Where does she live?	She lives in a house.
Where does he live?	He lives on a boat.
Do they live in a house now?	No, they live in a condo.
Do you live in a hotel?	No, we live in a tent.

Simple Past of *to live*

Where did you live before?	I lived in a house.
Where did you live?	We lived in a trailer.
Did they live in a condo?	No, they lived in a house.
Where did she live?	She lived in a castle.
Where did he live?	He lived in a castle, too.

Simple Past of *to be*
I was. He was. She was. It was.
We were. You were. They were.

WORD CHECKOUT

Please check yourself.
Fill in the spaces below. Write about yourself.

1. I am from _____.

2. I lived in a/an _____ before.

3. I live in a/an _____ now.

4. My home is _____.

WORDS "TO GO"

> Home sweet home.
> My home is my castle.

THE CARD SHOP

Home is where you hang your hat.

Congratulations on your new home.

LESSON 4
Say when...

Please talk about the picture.

1. What time is it in the picture?

2. Is the hand saying, "More, please" or "That's enough"?

READING 1

When do you get up?

When do you get up?

    With the sun?

    With the birds?

    When?

When do you go to bed?

    When the stars and moon are in the sky?

    With the cows?

    When?

When do you go to work?

When do you have fun?

Please talk about Reading 1.

1. When are the stars and moon in the sky?

2. Does the sun really "get up"?

3. Do birds "get up" early or late?

4. Do cows "go to bed" early or late?

Please talk about yourself.

1. When do you get up every day?

2. When do you go to bed every day?

3. Do you get up late sometimes? On weekends?

4. When do you have fun?

THE WORD BASKET

Here is a way to learn new words. Use these five steps.

STEP 1: Go back to Reading 1. Read it again. Find the words you want to remember. Write them in the spaces below:

New Words

1. _____
2. _____
3. _____
4. _____
5. _____
6. _____
7. _____
8. _____
9. _____
10. _____

STEP 2: Say your new words to the class. Your classmates will say their new words. Do you want to add other new words? Do it here:

Other New Words

_____

_____

STEP 3: Work with the class. Find out the meanings of your words. Write the new words and their meanings in English (or in your language) in the spaces below:

New Words   **Meanings**

1. _____   _____

2. _____   _____

3. _____   _____

4. _____   _____

5. _____   _____

6. _____   _____

7. _____   _____

8. _____   _____

9. _____   _____

10. _____   _____

Other New Words

_____   _____

_____   _____

STEP 4: Go back to Reading 1. Read it again. Now look at the list of **Target Words** for this lesson on page 129 of the Learning Guide. Do you want to change your list? Do that now.

STEP 5: Use your lists to help you remember your new words. Use these same five steps for Reading 2.

READING 2

Night or day?

My name is Olga Rejek. I sleep all day. I don't get up with the birds or the sun. I get up at three in the afternoon.

I get up when my family is home from school or work. What do we do? We talk. We study or read. We watch TV. We eat. We go out. We have fun.

Then I go to work. I go to work at 7 P.M. I work in a hotel. I work at night. I work on week nights.

Weekends are difficult for me. My family is ready to have fun on Saturdays and Sundays. When do I sleep on weekends? Night or day? Good question. What do you think?

Please talk about Reading 2.
Which sentences are true, and which sentences are false? Why?

1. Olga gets up with the sun.

2. She works in the morning.

3. She works at a hotel.

4. She has fun with her family.

Please write about it.
Write four true sentences about Olga. Use *she* in your sentences.

1. _____
2. _____
3. _____
4. _____

Please talk with family and friends.
Ask two or three friends when they work. Do they have problems with their work hours? Tell the class next time.

THE WORD STORE

Question Word: When?
When is the class?
When do I work?
When do you have fun?
When do we get up?
When do they sleep?
When does it get up?
When does she have fun?
When does he eat?

Simple Present: More Questions and Answers

Do you work?	Yes, I work at the hotel.
Do they have fun?	Yes, they have fun all day.
Do you sleep at night?	No, we work at night.
Does he get up early?	Yes, he gets up at 5 A.M.
Does she go to bed late?	No, she goes to bed at 10 P.M.
Does your cat get up early?	Yes, it gets up with the birds.

WORD CHECKOUT

Please check yourself.
Fill in the spaces below. Choose the best answer for you.

late   early   on weekends   at night   all day

1. I get up _____ on Mondays.

2. On weekends I get up _____ .

3. I work _____ .

4. I have fun _____ .

5. I go to bed _____ at night.

WORDS "TO GO"

> The early bird catches the worm.
> Better late than never.

THE CARD SHOP

LESSON 5

Why?... Why not!

Please talk about the picture.

1. What does the picture "say"?
2. What words do these letters "say": B C R T U ?

READING 1

Why am I here?

Why am I here…in the world? What are the reasons?

    To be?

    To be part of a family?

    To be part of a community?

    To be…me?

Why are we all here…in class? What are the reasons?

    To study and learn?

    To listen and talk?

    To read and write?

    To try new things?

    To make new friends?

Why? Why not!

Please talk about Reading 1.

1. Why are people here in the world?

2. What is a *community*?

3. What does it mean "to be…me?"

4. Name some reasons to be in class.

5. What are some other reasons to study?

Please talk about yourself.

1. What community are you part of?

2. Is it important to you to be part of a community? Why? Why not?

3. What do you want to learn in this class?

4. Why are you in this class?

THE WORD BASKET

Here is a way to learn new words. Use these five steps.

STEP 1: Go back to Reading 1. Read it again. Find the words you want to remember. Write them in the spaces below:

New Words

1. _____
2. _____
3. _____
4. _____
5. _____
6. _____
7. _____
8. _____
9. _____
10. _____

STEP 2: Say your new words to the class. Your classmates will say their new words. Do you want to add other new words? Do it here:

Other New Words

_____

_____

STEP 3: Work with the class. Find out the meanings of your words. Write the new words and their meanings in English (or in your language) in the spaces below:

New Words   **Meanings**

1. _____   _____

2. _____   _____

3. _____   _____

4. _____   _____

5. _____   _____

6. _____   _____

7. _____   _____

8. _____   _____

9. _____   _____

10. _____   _____

Other New Words

_____   _____

_____   _____

STEP 4: Go back to Reading 1. Read it again. Now look at the list of **Target Words** for this lesson on page 129 of the Learning Guide. Do you want to change your list? Do that now.

STEP 5: Use your lists to help you remember your new words. Use these same five steps for Reading 2.

READING 2

Why are you here?

Why am *I* here? First, I come to class to learn. I am here to speak, to read, and to write English. Second, I'm here to make new friends. I like people. Third, I want to get a diploma. A diploma is important in the world today.

Talk to my family about this class! Ask my daughter about the teacher. Ask my father about the students. They all know the lesson too! Wow! All day before class I study the lesson. My son says the words to me and I write them. We do the Readings, the questions, and the Word Store. We really think about those questions! Here's a question for you: Why are we here in the world? Wow! Here's my answer: Why not?

Please talk about Reading 2.

1. Why do people go to classes?

2. What is a *diploma*?

3. Is a diploma important? Why? Why not?

4. What does the writer do all day before class?

5. Talk about this question: "Why are we here in the world?"

Please write about it.
List the reasons you are in this class:

1. _____

2. _____

3. _____

4. _____

Please talk with family and friends.
Do your family and friends study too? Why do they study? Ask them. Tell the class the answers next time.

THE WORD STORE

Question Word: *Why?*
Why are you in the class?
Why do you study?

Negative sentences with *not* and *Why not?*
not = *n't*

I don't study.	Why not?
(I don't study because)	I work all day and all night.
She doesn't study.	Why not?
(She doesn't study because)	she sleeps all day and all night.

to + verb
Use *to* + a verb to tell the reason why.

Why do you study	(I study) to learn.
Why are you in the class?	(I'm in the class) to study English.
Why do you study English?	(I study English) to get a diploma.

WORD CHECKOUT

Please check yourself.
Circle the answers that are true for you. Talk about each answer with the class. If your answer is *yes*, tell why. If your answer is *no*, tell why not.

1. This class is fun for me.   Yes / No
2. I like to try new things.   Yes / No
3. I like to read.   Yes / No
4. I like to write.   Yes / No
5. I study at home.   Yes / No
6. I study at work.   Yes / No
7. I study with friends.   Yes / No

WORDS "TO GO"

> Some people dream and they ask, "Why"?
> I dream and I ask, "Why not"?
> —Robert Kennedy

THE CARD SHOP

Why read?
Why write?
Why study?

To graduate!
To graduate!
To graduate!
Congratulations on your diploma!

PART TWO

From Today to Tomorrow

PART TWO of this book is about everyday things. You will read and talk about:

>food,

>feeling sick,

>going to the doctor,

>looking for a new place to live,

>and

>finding a job.

Each lesson in the rest of the book is a little longer than the lessons in Part One.

LESSON 6

What is good to eat?

Please talk about the picture.

1. What are the people eating?

2. What time is it?

READING 1

The Five Food Groups

1. **The Bread Group**

   —includes all breads, cereals, rice, pasta, beans, and starchy vegetables like potatoes.

2. **The Meat Group**

   —includes meats, fish, eggs, and cheese.

3. **The Vegetable/Fruit Group**

   —includes all fruits and most vegetables except beans, corn, squash, and potatoes.

4. **The Milk Group**

   —includes milk and yogurt.

5. **The "F" Group**

   —includes foods (from all the other groups) that are high in FAT. Examples are avocados, mayonnaise, nuts, oils, butter, bacon, cream, and some cheeses.

Please talk about Reading 1.

1. Tell what you know about the five food groups.

2. Is eating from each group important? Why? Why not?

3. Do you know other food groups?

4. What happens when people eat too much fat?

Please talk about yourself.

1. How many times a day do you eat?

2. Where do you eat?

3. Do you eat alone or with other people?

4. What are some of your favorite foods?

THE WORD BASKET

Here is a way to learn new words. Use these five steps.

STEP 1: Go back to Reading 1. Read it again. Find the words you want to remember. Write them in the spaces below:

New Words

1. _____
2. _____
3. _____
4. _____
5. _____
6. _____
7. _____
8. _____
9. _____
10. _____

STEP 2: Say your new words to the class. Your classmates will say their new words. Do you want to add other new words? Do it here:

Other New Words

_____

_____

STEP 3: Work with the class. Find out the meanings of your words. Write the new words and their meanings in English (or in your language) in the spaces below:

New Words   **Meanings**

1. _____   _____

2. _____   _____

3. _____   _____

4. _____   _____

5. _____   _____

6. _____   _____

7. _____   _____

8. _____   _____

9. _____   _____

10. _____   _____

Other New Words

_____   _____

_____   _____

STEP 4: Go back to Reading 1. Read it again. Now look at the list of **Target Words** for this lesson on page 130 of the Learning Guide. Do you want to change your list? Do that now.

STEP 5: Use your lists to help you remember your new words. Use these same five steps for Reading 2.

READING 2

Really G-o-o-o-o-d Food

Nutritionists are people who study food. Then they tell us what to eat. They also tell us what food is not good. They tell us not to eat too much fat, salt, or sugar. But can they tell us what really tastes good? You know what I mean, don't you? Really tasty food is often salty or sweet. Or else it's full of fat.

For example, I looked again at those first four food groups. I didn't see cookies, potato chips, or hot dogs. Where's the ice cream? That's right. They're in the "F" group.

Did you eat something yesterday that was really, really good? What was it?

Now answer this question: Did this food contain fat, sugar, or salt? Tell the truth!

Please talk about Reading 2.
1. Say this word: "G-o-o-o-o-d." What word is it really?
2. What do nutritionists tell us?
3. Are foods in the "F group" good? Why? Why not?
4. What food did you eat yesterday that was really good? Tell why.

Please write about it.
Write one food from each group that you ate yesterday:

Bread: _____

Meat: _____

Fruit/Vegetable: _____

Milk: _____

Foods from your list that are high in fat:

_____

Please talk with family and friends.
Do your friends and family think about food groups? Ask them their ideas about good food. Tell the class next time.

THE WORD STORE

Review: The Simple Present: *he/she/it* + verb + *-s*

The verb in the simple present always ends in *s* when the subject is *he, she, it,* or a singular noun (name of a person, place, or thing).

He **is** important.
She **works** at night.
It **contains** fat.
Some cheese **has** a lot of salt.
My father **gets** up early.
Miss Smith **teaches** English.
Does Mr. Kim **like** meat?
Does this cat **eat** fish?
He **likes** vegetables.
Who **cooks** at your house?

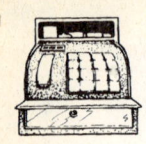

WORD CHECKOUT

Please check yourself.
Mark each food in the chart below with the correct food group. Also mark it "F" if it is high in fat.

Bread   Meat   Vegetable/Fruit   Milk

Food	Group	High in Fat?
1. Yogurt	_____	_____
2. Apples	_____	_____
3. Spaghetti	_____	_____
4. Hot dogs	_____	_____
5. Lettuce	_____	_____

WORDS "TO GO"

An apple a day keeps the doctor away.
I scream, you scream, we all scream for ice cream!

THE CARD SHOP

LESSON 7

How are you feeling?

Please talk about the picture.

1. How is the person on the sofa feeling?
2. What is the other person doing?

READING 1

Tender, Loving Care: Three Phone Calls

"I have the flu.

I have a stomachache too.

I'm going home to bed. I'm feeling sick."

    "There, there."

"I fell in the hall.

I banged my knee.

I need you, Mom. "

    "OK. I'm coming right away."

"I have the flu. I banged my knee.

I went to bed. I drank some tea.

My mom's here with her TLC.

I still feel rotten, Doctor.

What can I do?

    "Take two pills and call me in the morning."

Please talk about Reading 1.

1. What is *TLC*?

2. How is the sick person feeling?

3. Who said, "There, there?"

4. Who said, "OK. I'm coming right away?"

5. Who said, "Take two pills and call me in the morning?"

6. Talk about these words: *banged, fell, went, drank*.

Please talk about yourself.

1. What do you do for the flu?

2. What do you do if you can't sleep?

3. What is important to you when you are sick?

4. How do you know when it's time to call a doctor or go to the hospital?

THE WORD BASKET

Here is a way to learn new words. Use these five steps.

STEP 1: Go back to Reading 1. Read it again. Find the words you want to remember. Write them in the spaces below:

New Words

1. _____
2. _____
3. _____
4. _____
5. _____
6. _____
7. _____
8. _____
9. _____
10. _____

STEP 2: Say your new words to the class. Your classmates will say their new words. Do you want to add other new words? Do it here:

Other New Words

_____

_____

STEP 3: Work with the class. Find out the meanings of your words. Write the new words and their meanings in English (or in your language) in the spaces below:

New Words　　　　　　　　　**Meanings**

1. _____　　_____

2. _____　　_____

3. _____　　_____

4. _____　　_____

5. _____　　_____

6. _____　　_____

7. _____　　_____

8. _____　　_____

9. _____　　_____

10. _____　　_____

Other New Words

_____　　_____

_____　　_____

STEP 4: Go back to Reading 1. Read it again. Now look at the list of **Target Words** for this lesson on page 130 of the Learning Guide. Do you want to change your list? Do that now.

STEP 5: Use your lists to help you remember your new words. Use these same five steps for Reading 2.

READING 2

Our teacher isn't feeling very well...

For two weeks our teacher didn't come to class. She called in sick. She also wrote us this letter and asked us to write back.

Dear Class,

I'm sorry I can't be with you. I have the flu, and my doctor said, "Stay in bed." Well, I can't get out of bed. That's because I banged my knee last night.

Yesterday I felt really rotten. I had a sore throat and a fever. I ached all over.

Today I'm feeling better, but I'm not going out. My mother is taking care of me.

I'll see you next week, I hope. Please write to me.

                      Your teacher

Please talk about Reading 2.
Which sentences are true, and which sentences are false? Why?

1. The teacher didn't call the school.

2. She talked to the class.

3. Her mother said, "Stay in bed."

4. She's hoping to return next week.

Please write about it.
Write a note to this poor teacher. Look at the card from the class on page 60 for some good ideas.

Please talk with family and friends.
Some people think chicken soup can help you feel better when you have the flu. Other people have different ideas. Ask your family and friends what they do for the flu. Tell the class next time.

THE WORD STORE

Question Word: *How?*
How are you feeling?

Present Progressive tense: *am/is/are* + verb + *-ing*
Use this tense to tell what is *happening* now. Here are some examples from the Readings. Go back to the Readings and find more examples.

How are you feeling today? I'm feeling rotten.
I'm going home.
I'm coming right away.

Irregular Simple Past Tense
Some verbs have irregular past forms. They do not end with *-ed*.

to be	was/were	to fall	fell
to do	did	to feel	felt
to eat	ate	to go	went
to drink	drank	to say	said
to have	had	to write	wrote

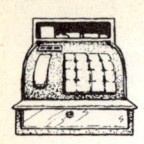

WORD CHECKOUT

Please check yourself.
Tell what you do when you're sick. Choose all the answers that are true for you, or tell a different answer.

1. When I have a sore throat, I: (a) do nothing   (b) drink a lot of water   (c) take pills   (d) stay in bed   (e) other (tell what)
2. When I have a stomachache, I: (a) do nothing   (b) stop eating   (c) take pills   (d) stay in bed   (e) other (tell what)
3. When I have the flu, I: (a) do nothing   (b) drink a lot of water   (c) take pills   (d) stay in bed   (e) other (tell what)
4. When I bang my knee, I: (a) do nothing   (b) put ice on it   (c) take pills   (d) stay in bed   (e) other (tell what)

WORDS "TO GO"

> There, there.
> I'm feeling under the weather.

THE CARD SHOP

LESSON 8

It's an emergency!

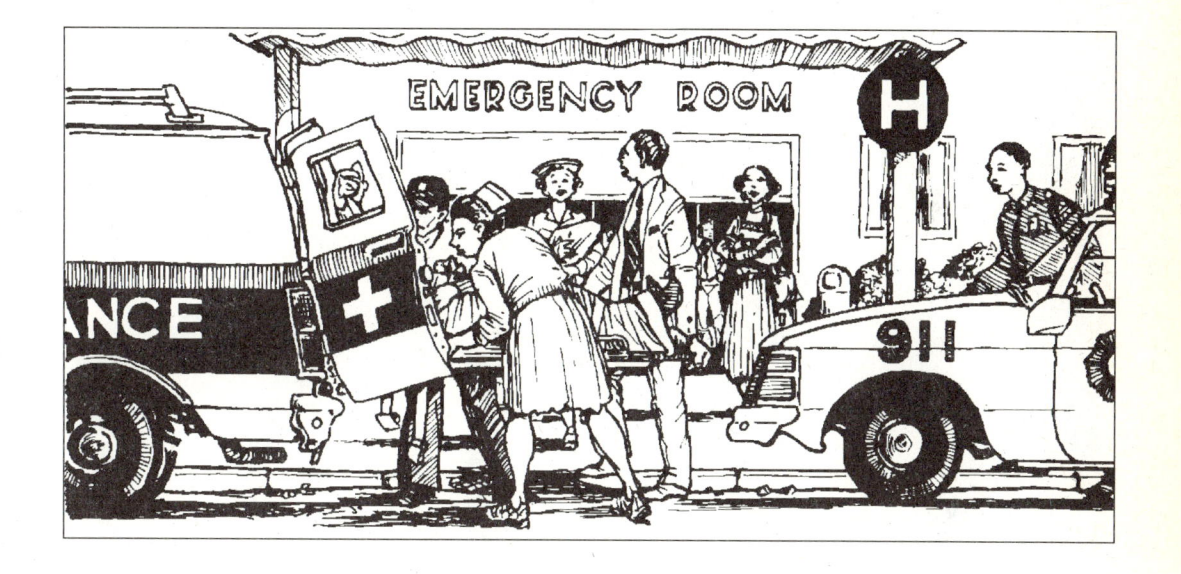

Please talk about the picture.

1. When do you call "911"?

2. What does the (red) cross mean?

3. What is an *emergency*?

READING 1

Emergency Room Form

If you go to a hospital Emergency Room, you will get a form with these questions:

Name: _Nicole Nadeau_

Address: _3 Randolph Rd., Centerville_

Phone: _555-3050_

Social Security Number: _123-45-6789_

Date of birth: _01-15-87_

Medical insurance: _Community_   Number: _007368_

Name any drugs you are allergic to: _penicillin_

I consent to treatment. Sign here: _Jeanne Nadeau_
                                      (mother)

Please talk about Reading 1.

1. What is a Social Security Number?

2. Why does the Emergency Room need this number?

3. Why does the Emergency Room need a date of birth?

4. What is *medical insurance*?

5. What does *allergic* mean?

6. What does *consent to treatment* mean?

Please talk about yourself.

1. Have you been to a hospital Emergency Room? Tell about it.

2. Where do you go for treatment if it's not an emergency?

3. What do you like about hospitals?

4. What do you dislike about hospitals?

THE WORD BASKET

Here is a way to learn new words. Use these five steps.

STEP 1: Go back to Reading 1. Read it again. Find the words you want to remember. Write them in the spaces below:

New Words

1. _____
2. _____
3. _____
4. _____
5. _____
6. _____
7. _____
8. _____
9. _____
10. _____

STEP 2: Say your new words to the class. Your classmates will say their new words. Do you want to add other new words? Do it here:

Other New Words

_____

_____

STEP 3: Work with the class. Find out the meanings of your words. Write the new words and their meanings in English (or in your language) in the spaces below:

New Words **Meanings**

1. _____   _____

2. _____   _____

3. _____   _____

4. _____   _____

5. _____   _____

6. _____   _____

7. _____   _____

8. _____   _____

9. _____   _____

10. _____   _____

Other New Words

_____   _____

_____   _____

STEP 4: Go back to Reading 1. Read it again. Now look at the list of **Target Words** for this lesson on page 131 of the Learning Guide. Do you want to change your list? Do that now.

STEP 5: Use your lists to help you remember your new words. Use these same five steps for Reading 2.

READING 2

In the Emergency Room

"We have to see a doctor. My daughter's leg is bleeding," said Nicole's mother.

The nurse answered, "OK. Fill out this form and then be seated, please."

They waited and waited and waited. Finally the doctor came.

"Well, young lady, what happened to you?" asked the doctor.

"I cut my leg," answered Nicole.

"Let's see," said the doctor. "Oh. You need two or three stitches. First I have to clean the cut."

"Will it hurt?" asked Nicole.

"Just hang on. I'll try to be quick," answered the doctor. "How did you do this?"

"I was climbing a fence. Ow! I fell. Ow!!" cried Nicole.

"All finished," said the doctor. "Next time, use the gate! Come back in a week, and I'll take the stitches out!"

"Thank you. Goodbye," said Nicole.

Please talk about Reading 2.

1. What happened to Nicole?

2. What did her mother do?

3. What did the doctor do?

4. What did the doctor tell Nicole?

Please write about it.
Here is the Emergency Room form again. Fill it out with information about yourself.

Name: _____

Address: _____

Phone: _____

Social Security Number: _____

Date of birth: _____

Medical insurance: _____ Number: _____

Name any drugs you are allergic to: _____

I consent to treatment. Sign here: _____

Please talk with family and friends.
Do your family or friends have stories about emergencies? Ask them and tell the class next time.

THE WORD STORE

Contraction: *let's = let us*
Let's see.   "Let's see the cut, Nicole."
Let's go.   "Let's go in the ambulance."

Possession: ' + s
Nicole's leg   (her leg)
Nicole's mother   (her mother)
Nicole's doctor   (her doctor)

Future Tense with *will*
will = 'll
You'll need two or three stitches.
Will it hurt?
I'll try to be quick.

WORD CHECKOUT

Please check yourself.
You're the doctor. Choose an answer and write the letter in the blank, or write a different answer.

____ 1. "My baby has a fever."

____ 2. "I have a bad stomachache."

____ 3. "My husband has a sore throat."

____ 4. "I can't sleep."

____ 5. "My friend fell and can't get up."

a. send an ambulance

b. take some medicine and lie down

c. wait and see

d. go to the hospital

e. try a cool bath

WORDS TO "GO"

A stitch in time saves nine.
Don't fence me in.

THE CARD SHOP

Good thing the doc could stitch you up!

Now you're a happy pup!

LESSON 9

There's no place like home...

Please talk about the picture.

1. Talk about the words on the sign.

2. What does *open house* mean?

3. Can any person look at a house for sale at an open house?

4. Have you ever looked at a house for sale?

READING 1

House Hunting

You need a place to live. Maybe you're buying a house, maybe you want to rent.

Who do you ask? A friend? A person at work? A person in your family?

Do you look in the newspaper for real estate ads? Well, that's OK.

But how about calling a realtor? Realtors can find you a house or apartment to buy or to rent. Finding places for people to live is their job. Look for their names and telephone numbers in the Real Estate section of the yellow pages of the telephone book.

Please talk about Reading 1.

1. What are some ways to find a new place to live?

2. Where can you find real estate ads?

3. Whose job is finding places for people to live?

4. Where can you find the names and telephone numbers of realtors?

Please talk about yourself.

1. How did you find the place you live in now?

2. How can you find a good realtor?

3. Do you own or rent your home now?

THE WORD BASKET

Here is a way to learn new words. Use these five steps.

STEP 1: Go back to Reading 1. Read it again. Find the words you want to remember. Write them in the spaces below:

New Words

1. _____
2. _____
3. _____
4. _____
5. _____
6. _____
7. _____
8. _____
9. _____
10. _____

STEP 2: Say your new words to the class. Your classmates will say their new words. Do you want to add other new words? Do it here:

Other New Words

_____

_____

STEP 3: Work with the class. Find out the meanings of your words. Write the new words and their meanings in English (or in your language) in the spaces below:

New Words **Meanings**

1. _____   _____

2. _____   _____

3. _____   _____

4. _____   _____

5. _____   _____

6. _____   _____

7. _____   _____

8. _____   _____

9. _____   _____

10. _____   _____

Other New Words

_____   _____

_____   _____

STEP 4: Go back to Reading 1. Read it again. Now look at the list of **Target Words** for this lesson on page 132 of the Learning Guide. Do you want to change your list? Do that now.

STEP 5: Use your lists to help you remember your new words. Use these same five steps for Reading 2.

READING 2

Real Estate Ads

Help me choose a new place to live. I am married with two children. We have two cars. Oh, yes…and a dog. We can pay $1,200.00 a month for rent, plus heat. We have good jobs. We think two of the places below look pretty good. Can you help us choose?

A

4 rm apt
new kit & bath
1 car pkg
no pets $750 mo htd
re: 555-9701

B

7 rm 3 bdrm apt
new bath   nice porch
yard   2 car pkg
pets OK
$950 mo unhtd
re: 111-1481

C

lge 1 rm effic
w/w   a/c
no pkg   nr pub transp
no pets
$550 mo htd
call: 555-0816

D

9 rm hse   4 bdrm
yard/pool
new bath/kit
central ac
2 car pkg
$1300 mo htd
re: 111-0121

Please talk about Reading 2.

1. Talk about the abbreviated words. Look at the list in the Word Store.

2. Which place is best for the family to live? Why?

3. What's the next best choice? Why?

Please write about it.
Here is a full description of Apartment A from Reading 2. Read it; then write a full description of Apartment B.

4 rm apt	Four-room apartment
new kit & bath	New kitchen and bathroom
1 car pkg	One-car parking
no pets $750 mo htd	No pets. $750 a month, heated
re: 555-9701	Realtor: 555-9701

Please talk with family and friends.
Ask people you know if it's better to own or rent a home, and why. Tell the class about it next time.

THE WORD STORE

Idioms with *for*
for sale
for rent

Abbreviations in Housing Ads
ac = a/c = air conditioning
ad = advertisement
apt = apartment
bath = bathroom
bdrm = bedroom
effic = efficiency apartment
furn = furnished
htd = heated
kit = kitchen
lge = large
rm = room
unhtd = unheated
w/w = wall-to-wall carpet

WORD CHECKOUT

Please check yourself.
True or false? Mark "T" for true or "F" for false.

____ 1. Apt means apartment.

____ 2. A realtor's job is to find friends for you.

____ 3. Bdrm means bathroom.

____ 4. *For sale* is the same as *for rent*.

____ 5. Newspapers have real estate ads.

WORDS "TO GO"

> Home at last.
> Call home.

THE CARD SHOP

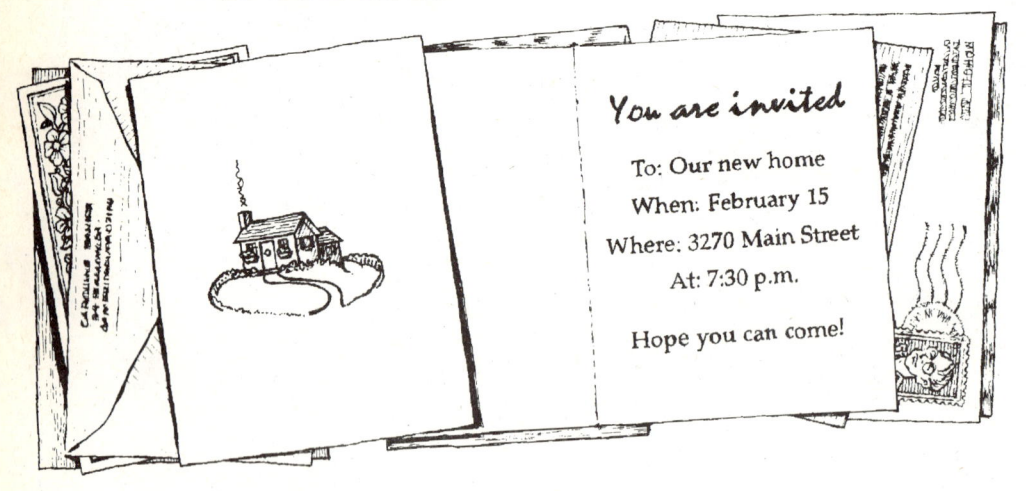

You are invited

To: Our new home
When: February 15
Where: 3270 Main Street
At: 7:30 p.m.

Hope you can come!

LESSON 10
Help Wanted

Please talk about the picture.
Read the sign about the job and talk about it.

1. What information is on the sign?

2. What important information is not on the sign?

3. What can you do to get more information about the job?

READING 1

Classified Advertising—Index

Looking for a job can be a full-time job. How can you begin? One way is to buy a copy of a newspaper and turn to the Classified Advertising section. Usually there is an Index at the beginning of the section. The name of each group of jobs is on this list. You can also advertise yourself in the Classified Advertising. Someone may read about you and call you for an interview. Here is the Index from a recent American newspaper:

Employment

Employment Wanted

Health Care Positions

Help Wanted A–Z

Part-Time Help Wanted

Please talk about Reading 1.

1. What section of the newspaper contains lists of jobs?

2. What's another word for *employment*?

3. What's another word for *position*?

4. What's the difference between "Help Wanted" and "Employment Wanted"?

5. What are "Health Care" jobs?

6. How many hours do you think is "part-time"?

Please talk about yourself.

1. Did you ever look for a job in the "Classified" section of a newspaper?

2. Did you ever find a job from a "Help Wanted" sign?

3. What are some other good ways to find a job?

THE WORD BASKET

Here is a way to learn new words. Use these five steps.

STEP 1: Go back to Reading 1. Read it again. Find the words you want to remember. Write them in the spaces below:

New Words

1. _____

2. _____

3. _____

4. _____

5. _____

6. _____

7. _____

8. _____

9. _____

10. _____

STEP 2: Say your new words to the class. Your classmates will say their new words. Do you want to add other new words? Do it here:

Other New Words

_____

_____

STEP 3: Work with the class. Find out the meanings of your words. Write the new words and their meanings in English (or in your language) in the spaces below:

New Words **Meanings**

1. _____ _____

2. _____ _____

3. _____ _____

4. _____ _____

5. _____ _____

6. _____ _____

7. _____ _____

8. _____ _____

9. _____ _____

10. _____ _____

Other New Words

_____ _____

_____ _____

STEP 4: Go back to Reading 1. Read it again. Now look at the list of **Target Words** for this lesson on page 132 of the Learning Guide. Do you want to change your list? Do that now.

STEP 5: Use your lists to help you remember your new words. Use these same five steps for Reading 2.

READING 2

Help Wanted A–Z

Here is part of a list of jobs from a newspaper. Read it and look for the names of jobs you know. Are you qualified for any of these jobs?

A
Airport security manager
Apartment manager
Autobody repair person

B
Baker
Bank teller
Bartender

C
Cashier
Child care provider
Construction worker
Cook

D
Day care provider
Delivery person
Driver — license required

F
Furniture mover — license required

G
Guard

H
Hair stylist
Health care aide
Hotel housekeeper

J
Janitor

L
Laborer
Landscaper

M
Maintenance person

N
Nurse

S
Secretary

W
Waitperson
Warehouse worker

Please talk about Reading 2.
1. Tell what you know about two or three of these jobs.
2. Name some jobs that are not in the Classified Ads.
3. Which jobs require a driver's license?
4. Which jobs require speaking English?
5. Which jobs require reading and writing English?

Please write about it.

1. Do you have a job? What is it?
2. What are the good and bad things about your job?
3. Are you looking for a job or a different job? Why?
4. Tell what jobs you can do.
5. Tell about a job you had in the past.
6. What is your "dream" job? Do you need English for this job?

Please talk with family and friends.
Find out how other people have looked for jobs. Tell the class about it next time.

THE WORD STORE

Alphabetical Order

Classified ads list jobs in alphabetical order, from A to Z. When two words begin with the same letter, the words are alphabetized from the second letter:

    D**a**y care provider
    D**e**livery person

When the first and second letters are the same, the words are alphabetized from the third letter:

    Co**n**struction worker
    Co**o**k

Look for other examples in the classified ads in Reading 2.

Put the following jobs in alphabetical order:

1. ____ apartment manager   2. ____ bartender

   ____ autobody repair person   ____ baker

   ____ airport security manager   ____ bank teller

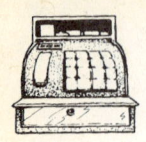

WORD CHECKOUT

Please check yourself.
True or false? Mark "T" for true or "F" for false.

____ 1. "Help wanted" and "Employment wanted" mean the same thing.

____ 2. A "health care position" is an aide or a nurse.

____ 3. People in all of these jobs take care of people: health care aide, day care provider, child care provider.

____ 4. You need a driver's license to be an auto body worker.

WORDS "TO GO"

> Another day, another dollar.
> Get a job!

THE CARD SHOP

PART THREE

How do you like it here?

PART THREE of this book is about "here." You'll read and talk about:

    baseball,

    choosing what you want to buy,

    feelings about death,

    thoughts about love,

    and

    a new life.

LESSON 11

Take me out to the ball game...

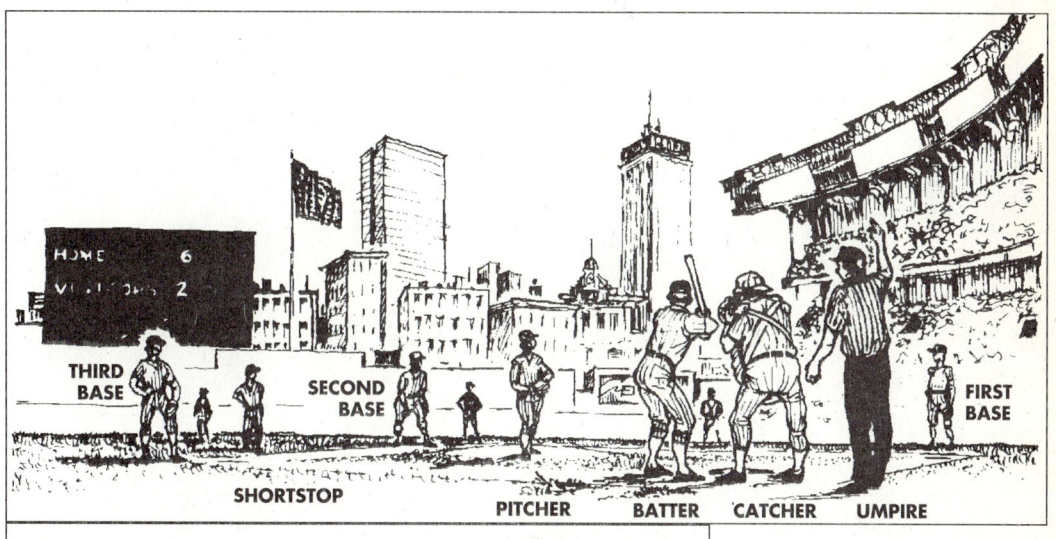

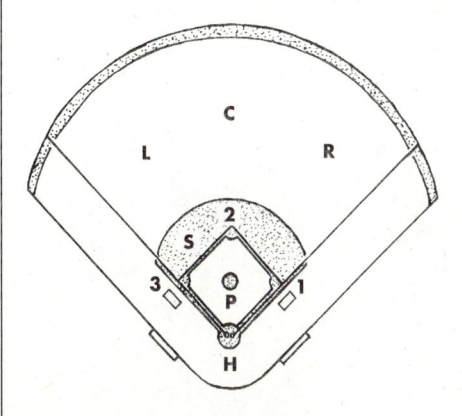

THIRD BASE — SHORTSTOP — SECOND BASE — PITCHER — BATTER — CATCHER — UMPIRE — FIRST BASE

HOME 6
VISITORS 2

- H HOME PLATE
- P PITCHER'S MOUND
- 1 FIRST BASE
- 2 SECOND BASE
- S SHORTSTOP
- 3 THIRD BASE
- L LEFT FIELD
- C CENTER FIELD
- R RIGHT FIELD

Please talk about the pictures.

1. What are these pictures about?

2. What are the people doing?

3. What is the score of the game?

READING 1

Play ball!

Baseball! Baseball!

America's pastime,

Played on a diamond

    field.

Batters to home plate,

Pitchers on the mound,

Umpires in the back:

    Game time.

4 bases to run,

9 innings to play,

3 strikes…YIKES!

    You're out.

A walk, a fly ball.

Single, double, triple.

It's a home run.

    You won!

Please talk about Reading 1.
Look again at the pictures on page 87.

1. What is this sport called?

2. Where does the pitcher stand?

3. How many strikes make an out?

4. Where does a batter stand?

5. What is a *home run*?

Please talk about yourself.

1. Do you like baseball? Why? Why not?

2. What other sports do you like?

3. Do you play a sport? Which one?

THE WORD BASKET

Here is a way to learn new words. Use these five steps.

STEP 1: Go back to Reading 1. Read it again. Find the words you want to remember. Write them in the spaces below:

New Words

1. _____

2. _____

3. _____

4. _____

5. _____

6. _____

7. _____

8. _____

9. _____

10. _____

STEP 2: Say your new words to the class. Your classmates will say their new words. Do you want to add other new words? Do it here:

Other New Words

_____

_____

STEP 3: Work with the class. Find out the meanings of your words. Write the new words and their meanings in English (or in your language) in the spaces below:

New Words **Meanings**

1. _____   _____

2. _____   _____

3. _____   _____

4. _____   _____

5. _____   _____

6. _____   _____

7. _____   _____

8. _____   _____

9. _____   _____

10. _____   _____

Other New Words

_____   _____

_____   _____

STEP 4: Go back to Reading 1. Read it again. Now look at the list of **Target Words** for this lesson on page 133 of the Learning Guide. Do you want to change your list? Do that now.

STEP 5: Use your lists to help you remember your new words. Use these same five steps for Reading 2.

READING 2

Baseball

Baseball is America's favorite pastime. There are nine baseball players on a team. And nine innings in a game. Some people say it is a slow sport. Sometimes a game can be three hours long. The games are often announced on the radio and shown on TV.

You may hear the announcer say things like these:

"It's the crack of the bat—

the crowd cheers—

it's the slide to home plate—

the throw—

too LATE!"

Baseball may be slow, but it's worth the wait.

Please talk about Reading 2.
1. What is America's favorite pastime.
2. Why is the number "9" important to baseball?
3. How many hours can a game be?
4. What does *worth the wait* mean?
5. What does *crack of the bat* mean?

Please write about it.
1. Do you like to watch sports on TV? Why? Why not?
2. Did you ever see a baseball game? When? Where? Who played?
3. Did you ever play baseball? What position did you play?
4. Which player is more exciting for you—the pitcher or the hitter? Why?
5. Who is usually right—the player or the umpire? Why?

Please talk with family and friends.
Ask your family and friends about their favorite pastimes. Do they like baseball? Do they watch the game or play it? Tell the class next time.

THE WORD STORE

Compound Words
Some words are made of two words. They are called *compound words*.

baseball = base + ball
pastime = pas(s) + time

Prepositions
A preposition is a word used with a noun or pronoun to show where, when, or how. The most common prepositions are: *of, at, on, in, to, from, with, for, out, about*. You may want to go back to other lessons and find more examples. Here are some prepositions from this lesson:

to the ball game
the score *of* the game
played *on* a diamond field
umpires *in* the back

Irregular Past Tense
to win   won

WORD CHECKOUT

Please check yourself.
True or false? Mark "T" for true or "F" for false.

____ 1. Baseball is a fast sport.

____ 2. There are nine innings in a game.

____ 3. The batter stands on the mound.

____ 4. Three strikes and you are out.

____ 5. The umpire catches the ball.

WORDS "TO GO"

> out in left field
> batting a thousand

THE CARD SHOP

THINKING OF YOU.

LET'S TOUCH BASE SOON.

LESSON 12
Too Many, Too Much

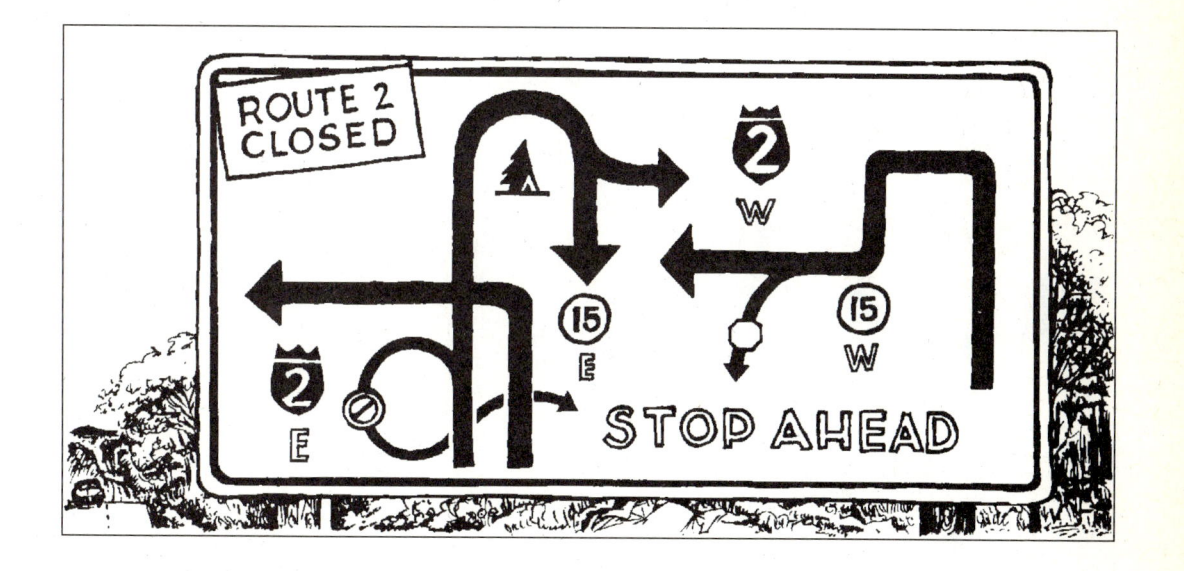

Please talk about the picture.

1. Talk about the words on the sign.

2. Why is the sign confusing?

3. Does the sign tell you the best way to go?

READING 1

1. Max is going to make himself a delicious tuna salad. First, he needs a can of tuna. But which one?

2. Max is getting confused and upset. He can't choose a can of tuna.

3. Max is going crazy. He can't deal with this situation.

4. Max is very, very hungry now. He has an idea.

5. Max will try again next week to make himself a delicious tuna salad. For now he needs food, any food, and fast!

Please talk about Reading 1.

1. Why does Max want to buy tuna?

2. How many kinds of canned tuna are at the supermarket?

3. Tell how Max feels in each picture.

4. What does Max do at the end of the story?

5. What's a good title for this story?

6. Talk about these words: *the can, the cans, can, can't, canned.*

Please talk about yourself.

1. Which is better—a supermarket or a small grocery store? Why?

2. Do you get confused about what to buy in a supermarket? Why?

3. Who do you ask for help in a supermarket?

4. Did you ever buy the wrong thing? What did you do?

THE WORD BASKET

Here is a way to learn new words. Use these five steps.

STEP 1: Go back to Reading 1. Read it again. Find the words you want to remember. Write them in the spaces below:

New Words

1. _____
2. _____
3. _____
4. _____
5. _____
6. _____
7. _____
8. _____
9. _____
10. _____

STEP 2: Say your new words to the class. Your classmates will say their new words. Do you want to add other new words? Do it here:

Other New Words

_____

_____

STEP 3: Work with the class. Find out the meanings of your words. Write the new words and their meanings in English (or in your language) in the spaces below:

New Words **Meanings**

1. _____   _____

2. _____   _____

3. _____   _____

4. _____   _____

5. _____   _____

6. _____   _____

7. _____   _____

8. _____   _____

9. _____   _____

10. _____   _____

Other New Words

_____   _____

_____   _____

STEP 4: Go back to Reading 1. Read it again. Now look at the list of **Target Words** for this lesson on page 133 of the Learning Guide. Do you want to change your list? Do that now.

STEP 5: Use your lists to help you remember your new words. Use these same five steps for Reading 2.

READING 2

A Note to Mom

Dear Mom,

I know you told me to eat right and to watch my cholesterol. Well, Mom, today I tried, believe me. Here's what happened.

I went to the supermarket and I found the canned tuna. But there were too many kinds. I couldn't make a decision. I stood there for about ten minutes. I got more and more confused and upset. Finally, I left the supermarket with
nothing. I just walked out.

I was so hungry I went to the fast food place and, well, you know the rest of the story.

My pet peeve about this country is this: There are too many choices! Can you tell me what kind of tuna to buy?

                         Love,

                         M a x

P.S. How much cholesterol is there in a triple cheeseburger, fries, and a shake?

Please talk about Reading 2.

1. There are seven irregular past verbs in Max's letter. Find them and talk about them.
2. What did Max's mom tell him to do? Why?
3. What does Max hate about this country?
4. What is a *triple cheeseburger*?
5. Do you think Max's story is funny, sad, or both?

Please write about it.
1. Do you eat right and watch your cholesterol?
2. Which contains more cholesterol—a cheeseburger or a tuna salad?
3. What do you think is a good kind of canned tuna?
4. What are your pet peeves about this country? Make a list and share it with the class.

Please talk with family and friends.
Ask your family and friends to tell you their pet peeves. Bring the list to class next time.

THE WORD STORE

too much / too many
Use *too much* with singular nouns. Use *too many* with plural nouns.
> There's too much food in a supermarket.
> There are too many choices.
> There were too many kinds.

could / couldn't
Could and *couldn't* are the past forms of *can* and *can't*.
> I could find the tuna yesterday, but there were too many kinds.
> I couldn't decide.

More Irregular Past Verbs
to be	was/were
to find	found
to get	got
to go	went
to leave	left
to stand	stood
to tell	told

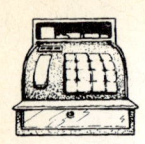

WORD CHECKOUT

Please check yourself.
Complete the sentences. There may be more than one good answer.

1. Max felt _____ in the supermarket.

2. Max left the supermarket with _____ .

3. Max bought _____ that day.

4. Max told his story to _____ .

WORDS "TO GO"

> Shop 'til you drop.
> Decisions, decisions!

THE CARD SHOP

LESSON 13

Loss

Please talk about the picture.

1. What is happening?

2. Do you feel comfortable talking about death? If you do, continue with the conversation.

3. Tell some of your funeral customs.

READING 1

The Black Dress

I arrived Tuesday night at 7:00. The students took their seats. I asked them to take out their assignments. The class began.

"Who can tell me the past tense of *take*?" I asked.

"*Took!*" they shouted.

"The past tense of *ring*?" I asked.

"*Rang!*" they all yelled.

Then I saw Aida. She was wearing a black dress, black shoes, black stockings, and a black sweater. Her eyes were looking down, and she was silent. Aida always knew the answers. She often was the first to put up her hand. That night she never spoke or looked up.

After class, I went over to her and asked her quietly, "Aida, what is wrong?"

Please talk about Reading 1.

1. What time did the class begin?

2. What was the class studying?

3. What was Aida wearing?

4. How did she feel?

5. Was Aida usually this way?

6. What do you think was wrong with Aida?

Please talk about yourself.

1. What do you say to someone who is looking and acting very sad?

2. Is it better to talk to someone right away, or to wait for a quiet moment?

3. What do black clothes mean to you?

THE WORD BASKET

Here is a way to learn new words. Use these five steps.

STEP 1: Go back to Reading 1. Read it again. Find the words you want to remember. Write them in the spaces below:

New Words

1. _____
2. _____
3. _____
4. _____
5. _____
6. _____
7. _____
8. _____
9. _____
10. _____

STEP 2: Say your new words to the class. Your classmates will say their new words. Do you want to add other new words? Do it here:

Other New Words

_____

_____

STEP 3: Work with the class. Find out the meanings of your words. Write the new words and their meanings in English (or in your language) in the spaces below:

New Words   **Meanings**

1. _____   _____

2. _____   _____

3. _____   _____

4. _____   _____

5. _____   _____

6. _____   _____

7. _____   _____

8. _____   _____

9. _____   _____

10. _____   _____

Other New Words

_____   _____

_____   _____

STEP 4: Go back to Reading 1. Read it again. Now look at the list of **Target Words** for this lesson on page 134 of the Learning Guide. Do you want to change your list? Do that now.

STEP 5: Use your lists to help you remember your new words. Use these same five steps for Reading 2.

READING 2

After Class

Aida began to cry.

"What's the matter?" I asked.

"My brother. He was my baby brother. He died."

"How old was he?" I asked.

"Fifty-two," she answered.

"Was he sick?" I asked.

"A heart attack," Aida cried.

"Oh, I'm so sorry, Aida. When did this happen?"

"Six days ago. He went to bed and died in his sleep."

"Oh, Aida. I am really sorry."

Aida had tears in her eyes. "I have one question…why *him*?"

Please talk about Reading 2.

1. What is a *heart attack*?

2. How old was Aida's brother when he died?

3. Why does Aida call him "baby brother"?

4. Did Aida's brother die peacefully? How do you know?

5. What does the teacher say to Aida?

Please write about it.
1. How would you answer Aida's question?
2. What can you say to a person who has had a death in the family?
3. Is it important to go to funerals?

Please talk with family and friends.
Ask about death and funeral customs. Do they send flowers and cards? Food? Money? Do they wear black clothes? What do they say to the family? Tell the class next time.

THE WORD STORE

Past Progressive Tense
Use *was/were* + verb + *-ing*.
> What was Aida wearing? She was wearing a black dress.
> Her eyes were looking down.

More Irregular Past Verbs
to know	knew
to ring	rang
to see	saw
to speak	spoke
to take	took

Fill in the blanks. Choose the best irregular past verb from the list above.

1. I _____ the doorbell.

2. They _____ on the telephone for an hour.

3. Aida usually _____ all the answers.

4. The students _____ their seats.

5. We _____ her black dress.

WORD CHECKOUT

Please check yourself.
True or false?

___ 1. Aida's brother died in a car accident.

___ 2. Aida was younger than her brother.

___ 3. Aida's brother died about a week ago.

___ 4. The teacher spoke to Aida quietly.

___ 5. Aida wore black because her brother died.

WORDS "TO GO"

> He/she passed away.
> We're thinking of you.

THE CARD SHOP

LESSON 14

Love

Please talk about the picture.

1. Who is in this picture?

2. What is he doing? Why?

3. What is love?

READING 1

Lucky in Love

Are you lucky or unlucky in love? We asked people this question, and here's what they said:

Paul: I am very lucky in love, I think. All the people I've loved have been very good people.

Mary: I am both lucky and unlucky. When I'm in love it's heaven. When it's over it's hell.

Nick: Both. Unlucky young. Lucky old. It was destiny.

Anne: Unlucky. He left because of another woman.

Liza: No, I'm not lucky. I've worked hard for all the love I've got. Luck has nothing to do with love.

Tom: Not unlucky. So far I haven't met *the* person.

Please talk about Reading 1.

1. What does being *in love* mean?

2. Do you think Paul is young, middle-aged, or old?

3. Do you think Tom is young or old? Why?

4. Does Liza believe in luck or not? How do you know?

5. Nick says destiny was important. What is *destiny*?

6. Which answers seem funny to you? Sad? True? Half-true?

Please talk about yourself.

1. Are you lucky in love? Why? Why not?

2. Which answer in Reading 1 is most like you? Tell why.

3. Do you think people can be too young or too old for love? Explain.

THE WORD BASKET

Here is a way to learn new words. Use these five steps.

STEP 1: Go back to Reading 1. Read it again. Find the words you want to remember. Write them in the spaces below:

New Words

1. _____
2. _____
3. _____
4. _____
5. _____
6. _____
7. _____
8. _____
9. _____
10. _____

STEP 2: Say your new words to the class. Your classmates will say their new words. Do you want to add other new words? Do it here:

Other New Words

_____

_____

STEP 3: Work with the class. Find out the meanings of your words. Write the new words and their meanings in English (or in your language) in the spaces below:

New Words   **Meanings**

1. _____   _____

2. _____   _____

3. _____   _____

4. _____   _____

5. _____   _____

6. _____   _____

7. _____   _____

8. _____   _____

9. _____   _____

10. _____   _____

Other New Words

_____   _____

_____   _____

STEP 4: Go back to Reading 1. Read it again. Now look at the list of **Target Words** for this lesson on page 134 of the Learning Guide. Do you want to change your list? Do that now.

STEP 5: Use your lists to help you remember your new words. Use these same five steps for Reading 2.

READING 2

Old Sweethearts

We met at a children's party. He was eleven and I was ten. I thought he was smart and funny, but not handsome. I don't know what he thought of me. We were just friends for many years.

One day, when we were about thirty, we met again at a party. We were both unhappy with our lives. After the party we walked and talked, and talked, and talked. Soon after, we discovered we loved each other and decided to be together. That was more than twenty-five years ago. We are happy old sweethearts.

Please talk about Reading 2.

1. Where did the sweethearts meet?
2. What did they think of each other then?
3. When did they meet again?
4. What did they discover?
5. Are they still together?

Please write about it.
1. Are you lucky or unlucky in love? Explain.
2. How old were you when you first fell in love?
3. Do you still think about an old sweetheart?
4. Name some places that make you think of love. Explain why.

Please talk with family and friends.
Ask some of your friends how they met and fell in love. When did it happen? Were they lucky or unlucky in love? Tell the class next time.

THE WORD STORE

The Prefix *un-*
Putting *un-* before some English words changes the meaning to the negative. *Un-* = not. Here are some examples from Lesson 14:

    un + lucky   unlucky = not lucky
    un + happy   unhappy = not happy

Fill in the blanks. Use *happy, unhappy, lucky,* or *unlucky*.

1. I found my book under the bed yesterday. That was _____ because we have a class today.

2. Friday the 13th is an _____ day in this country.

3. I have a wonderful family and a good job. I'm a _____ person.

4. "Why are you crying? You're not usually _____."

More Irregular Past Verbs
to meet   met
to think   thought

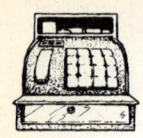

WORD CHECKOUT

Please check yourself.
True or false?

____ 1. All the people in Reading 1 were lucky in love.

____ 2. Liza thinks love comes with hard work.

____ 3. The "old sweethearts" in Reading 2 fell in love as children.

____ 4. They are about 35 years old now.

____ 5. They are happy now.

WORDS "TO GO"

> Love makes the world go round.
> All's fair in love and war.

THE CARD SHOP

Roses are red,
Violets are blue,
Sugar is sweet,
And so are you.

Be my Valentine.

LESSON 15

Life

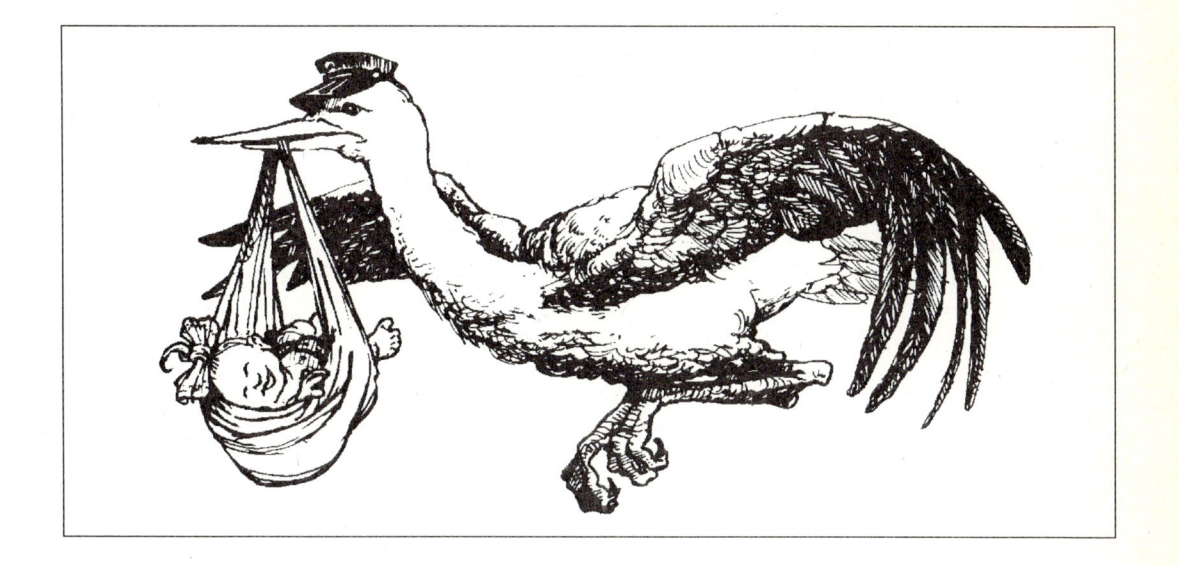

Please talk about the picture.

1. What is this picture about?

2. What is the bird doing?

3. Is this baby a girl or a boy? How do you know?

READING 1

A New Arrival

WHO?

  Susanna Hamilton

WHEN?

  On Sunday, June 15, at 3:43 A.M.

WHERE?

  At the Midwest Clinic

HOW MUCH?

  7 lbs. 3 ozs.

HOW LONG?

  19 in.

PROUD PARENTS:

  Kevin and Karen Hamilton

Please talk about Reading 1.

1. What is the baby's name?

2. When was she born?

3. Where was she born?

4. How much did she weigh?

5. How long is she?

Please talk about yourself.

1. Were you born in a hospital or at home?

2. Which is better—to be born in a hospital or at home?

3. What is your favorite name for a girl? For a boy?

THE WORD BASKET

Here is a way to learn new words. Use these five steps.

STEP 1: Go back to Reading 1. Read it again. Find the words you want to remember. Write them in the spaces below:

New Words

1. _____

2. _____

3. _____

4. _____

5. _____

6. _____

7. _____

8. _____

9. _____

10. _____

STEP 2: Say your new words to the class. Your classmates will say their new words. Do you want to add other new words? Do it here:

Other New Words

_____

_____

STEP 3: Work with the class. Find out the meanings of your words. Write the new words and their meanings in English (or in your language) in the spaces below:

New Words   **Meanings**

1. _____   _____

2. _____   _____

3. _____   _____

4. _____   _____

5. _____   _____

6. _____   _____

7. _____   _____

8. _____   _____

9. _____   _____

10. _____   _____

Other New Words

_____   _____

_____   _____

STEP 4: Go back to Reading 1. Read it again. Now look at the list of **Target Words** for this lesson on page 135 of the Learning Guide. Do you want to change your list? Do that now.

STEP 5: Use your lists to help you remember your new words. Use these same five steps for Reading 2.

READING 2

Special Delivery

Susanna Hamilton was born after midnight, in the wee hours of the morning. The doctors said this is a common time for deliveries. They also said Susanna's weight was average for baby girls. Her length was normal, too. Karen and Kevin didn't care if the baby was a boy or a girl. They just wanted a healthy child, and Susanna is very healthy.

Susanna's parents waited a long time for her—nine months. But the baby's grandparents waited even longer. They've been hoping for a grandchild for years. The whole family is thrilled by their little "special delivery."

Welcome, Susanna!

Please talk about Reading 2.

1. When was Susanna born?
2. What did the doctors say about Susanna's weight and length?
3. Did Karen and Kevin want a boy or did they want a girl?
4. How long have the baby's grandparents been waiting for her?
5. How does the whole family feel about the baby?

Please write about it.

1. When is your birthday?

2. What time of day were you born?

3. Where were you born?

4. How much did you weigh?

Please talk with family and friends.
Ask them to tell you their favorite names for a boy and a girl. Tell the class next time.

THE WORD STORE

Abbreviations
A.M. = ante meridien (before 12 o'clock noon)
P.M. = post meridien (after 12 o'clock noon)
lb./lbs. = pound/pounds
oz. = ounce/ounces
in. = inch/inches

Same Family / Different Job
Some words belong to the same family, but they do different jobs. The different jobs have different names—for example, nouns, verbs, adjectives. Here are some examples of words from the Readings. They are in the same family, but they do different jobs.

weight *(noun)*   The weight of a healthy baby is important.
to weigh *(verb)*   How much did Susanna weigh?

length *(noun)*   My length was 22 inches at birth.
long *(adjective)*   I was a very long baby.

birth *(noun)*   The birth of their granddaughter was thrilling.
to be born *(verb)*   She was born in the wee hours.

WORD CHECKOUT

Please check yourself.
A baby boy, Robert, was born at 4:30 P.M. on Tuesday, November 8 at the Downtown Hospital to Rita and Raymond Rico. Robert's weight at birth was 8 lbs. 7 oz., and his length was 20 in. Please complete his birth announcement:

Who? _____
When? _____
Where? _____
How much? _____ *How long?* _____
Proud parents: _____

WORDS "TO GO"

bundle of joy
the pitter patter of little feet

THE CARD SHOP

Learning Guide

LESSON 1 Who are you?
This lesson is about you, the student. You can tell the teacher and the other students about yourself. You can learn about the other students. You will practice asking and answering questions using the word *who*.

Word Basket: Target Words The target words are words in the lesson that may be new to you. Use this list with the WORD BASKET section of the lesson. The words are in the order they appear in the lesson.

Reading 1

who	voice	family	country	(Do you) like
my	words	work	more	
name	body	past	writer	
face	your	dreams	introduce	

Reading 2

| important | writer | (What does this) mean? |

Word Checkout There are no right or wrong answers to this exercise. Talk about your answers with the other students.

Words "To Go"
We are the world. = We are everybody. = We come from many places.
I think, therefore I am. = I can think. That means I am. = Thinking equals being.
  (Famous words by Descartes, a French philosopher.)

The Card Shop The person on the card looks like a famous statue by Auguste Rodin, a French sculptor. The statue is called "The Thinker." People send greeting cards just to say hello. You can find cards like this in the card section marked "Thinking of You."

LESSON 2 What's this book about?
This lesson is about your book, *Night & Day*. We hope you like it! It is also about you and your classmates. You will practice asking and answering questions using the word *what*.

Word Basket: Target Words

Reading 1

what	address	telephone number	house	full name
first	street	man	lives	
last	language	woman	learn	

Reading 2

only	alone	here	all (night)	OK
enters	feels	hmmm	page iii	begins
classroom	a little	cover	contents	
early	nervous	title	list	
sits down	night	day	alphabet	

Word Checkout   Answer about yourself.

Words "To Go"
What's it all about? = What is it really about? = What does it mean?
What's new? = What is new in your life? = Tell me the news about yourself.

The Card Shop   This party invitation is for all students. The invitation is on a bulletin board. You can also send invitations. Usually they are in packages in the party section of the card store. Some invitations are for special kinds of parties. Be sure to read the invitations before you buy them. You don't want to buy "baby shower" invitations if you are giving an "engagement" party!

LESSON 3   Where, oh where?

This lesson is about where you come from. It's about finding places on a map of the world. It's also about where you live now. It's about home. You will practice asking and answering questions using the word *where*.

Word Basket: Target Words
map

Reading 1

where	room	hotel	castle	now
oh	tent	apartment	boat	before
car	trailer	condo	coat	dream house

Reading 2

home	new	happy	same	eat
from	small	modern	place	very
different	lovely	comfortable	sleep	heart

Word Checkout
Answer about yourself.

Words "To Go"
Home sweet home. = Home is sweet. = Home is good.
My home is my castle. = I am the king (the boss) in my home. =
   My home is as good as a king's home.

The Card Shop
You "hang your hat" at home. Of course, you hang your coat there, too! You keep all your important things there. That makes a place "home."

LESSON 4   Say when...

This lesson is about time. It's about the things you do every day. You will practice asking and answering questions using the word *when*.

Word Basket: Target Words
when	what time	enough

Reading 1

get up	go to bed	sky	have fun	sometimes
sun	stars	cows	late	weekends
birds	moon	go to work	every (day)	

Reading 2

sleep	watch TV	(7) P.M.	ready
afternoon	eat	week (nights)	good
school	go out	difficult	think

Word Checkout   Answer about yourself.

Words "To Go"
The early bird catches the worm. = The bird that gets up early finds food to eat. (Birds eat worms.) = It's a good idea to be early, not late.
Better late than never. = It is better to be late than to be absent. = On time is good. Late is not very good. Late is better than nothing.

The Card Shop   Post cards are fun to send when you're on vacation or traveling. They are also fun to collect. Some people even collect old post cards with messages on them!

LESSON 5   Why? ... Why not?

This lesson is about some interesting "deep" questions. It is also about the reasons you want to learn. You will practice asking and answering questions using the word *why*.

Word Basket: Target Words
why	why not

Reading 1

world	part of	in class	learn	things
reasons	community	study	try	make (friends)

Reading 2

come	diploma	father	son	answer
second	today	know	says	
people	daughter	wow!	question	
third	teacher	all (day)	really	

Word Checkout   Answer about yourself.

Words "To Go"
Some people dream and they ask, "Why"? I dream and I ask, "Why not"? = Some people think they can't have their dream, but I think my dream is possible. = Other people are afraid to try new things. Not me. (Robert Kennedy was the brother of President John F. Kennedy.)

The Card Shop   *Congratulations* means "good for you"! There are many reasons to congratulate your family and friends. You will see a lot of different "congratulation" cards in the store. Be sure you find the right reason! *Congratulations on your retirement* is not the same as *Congratulations on your new job*!

LESSON 6 What is good to eat?

This lesson is about the food you eat. It's about eating the right foods every day. You will learn the names of the food groups.

Word Basket: Target Words

eat	eating	what time		

Reading 1

food	starchy	fruit	fat	bacon
group	vegetable(s)	corn	examples	cream
bread	potato(es)	squash	avocados	happens
cereal	meat	milk	mayonnaise	too much
rice	fish	yogurt	nuts	how many times
pasta	eggs	other	oils	(a day)
beans	cheese	high	butter	favorite

Reading 2

nutritionists	tasty	full of	potato chips	yesterday
salt	salty	for example	hot dogs	contain
sugar	sweet	again	ice cream	truth
tastes	or else	cookies	that's right	

Word Checkout

	Food	Group	High in Fat?
1.	Yogurt	*milk*	
2.	Apples	*fruit*	
3.	Spaghetti	*bread*	
4.	Hot dogs	*meat*	F
5.	Lettuce	*vegetable*	

Words "To Go"

An apple a day keeps the doctor away. = Eat one apple every day. You won't be sick. = Apples are good for you.

I scream, you scream, we all scream for ice cream! = Everybody likes ice cream.
   (To scream for = to say "Give me"!) Try saying this phrase very fast. Hint: *I scream* sounds like *ice cream.*

The Card Shop   Many people in North America really are too fat. Many more people think they are too fat. Trying to lose fat, or *dieting,* is big business. There even are cards for people trying to diet!

LESSON 7 How are you feeling?

This lesson is about feeling sick. It's also about feeling better!

Word Basket: Target Words

feeling	sofa	person	doing	

Reading 1

tender	stomachache	fell	went	morning
loving	sick	hall	drank	can't
care	"there, there"	need	TLC	doctor
phone calls	banged	Mom	rotten	hospital
flu	knee	right away	pills	

Reading 2

(feeling) well	dear	get out of	(all) over	hope
called in sick	sorry	because	better	poor
wrote	said	sore throat	but	chicken soup
letter	stay	fever	taking care of	
(write) back	well	ached	next	

Word Checkout   Answer about yourself.

Words "To Go"

There, there. = I'm sorry you feel bad. (Say these words in a soft and sweet voice. These words are usually for a person you love.)

I'm feeling under the weather. = I'm not feeling well. = I'm sick.

The Card Shop   This is a "get well" card from a group. The group can be friends from work, from school, or from a club, church, or other organization. You will also find group birthday cards. They are usually big. That way, everyone can write a message.

LESSON 8   It's an emergency!

This lesson is about emergencies: What you do, where you go, who you call.

Word Basket: Target Words

ambulance	emergency	(red) cross

Reading 1

emergency room	medical	allergic	treatment
form	insurance	penicillin	sign
Social Security	drugs	consent	dislike

Reading 2

leg	finally	Just hang on	Ow! (expression)
bleeding	cut	(expression)	gate
fill out	stitches	climbing	
be seated	hurt	fence	

Word Checkout   Answer for yourself.

Words "To Go"

A stitch in time saves nine. = Sew one stitch now, and maybe you won't need nine later. = Take care of a small problem before it becomes a big problem.

Don't fence me in. = Don't put me behind a fence. = Don't take away my freedom. = Don't try to stop me.

The Card Shop   This is a "get well" card. It could be sent to a person in the hospital.

Good thing = It's good that

Doc is a friendly, informal abbreviation for *doctor*. It is better not to use *doc* when you are speaking with your doctor.

Pup is a friendly abbreviation for *puppy*, a baby dog. A *happy puppy* (person) is no longer a *sick puppy* (person).

There are many kinds of "get well" cards. Some are friendly or funny like this one. If you don't want a funny card, be sure to ask the salesperson in the store to help you find the right one.

LESSON 9   There's no place like home ...

This lesson is about finding a place to live. Who do you talk to? What do you read? Where do you look?

Word Basket: Target Words

place	the sign	for sale	open house

Reading 1

hunting	newspaper	realtor	yellow pages
buying	real estate	finding	telephone book
rent	ads	section	own

Reading 2

help	month	pretty good	abbreviated
choose	plus	(See **Word Store**	best
married	heat	for abbreviations	next best
dog	jobs	in ads)	choice

Word Checkout
1. True   2. False   3. False   4. False   5. False

Words "To Go"
Home at last. = I am very happy to be home.
Call home. = Telephone your family.

The Card Shop   This is a "housewarming" card. Send a card like this to celebrate someone's new home. If you are invited to a "housewarming party," it is is nice to bring a present.

LESSON 10   Help Wanted

This lesson is about finding work. Where can you look? How do you begin?

Word Basket: Target Words

help	wanted	(the) sign	job	information

Reading 1

classified	copy	advertise	interview	positions
advertising	turn	yourself	recent	part-time
index	usually	someone	employment	
full-time	beginning	may	health care	

Reading 2

qualified	bartender	day care	guard	landscaper
airport security	cashier	delivery	hair stylist	maintenance
manager	child care	driver	aide	nurse
autobody repair	provider	license	housekeeper	secretary
baker	construction	required	janitor	waitperson
banker	cook	furniture mover	laborer	warehouse

Word Checkout
1. False   2. True   3. True   4. False

Words "To Go"
Another day, another dollar. = I worked a day and I got a little more money.
Get a job! = Stop sitting around the house with no money!

The Card Shop   You send a card like this when someone gets a new job or a better job.

LESSON 11   Take me out to the ball game ...
This lesson is about baseball rules and customs. Baseball is a very popular sport in America.

Word Basket: Target Words
ball game   score

Reading 1

baseball	pitchers	innings	a fly ball	sport
pastime	mound	strikes	single	stand
diamond	umpires	yikes!	double	
field	game time	(expression)	triple	
batters	bases	you're out	home run	
home plate	run	a walk	won	

Reading 2

favorite	(three hours) long	crack	throw	exciting
players	announced	bat	too late	
team	radio	crowd	worth the wait	
slow	shown	cheers	position (on a	
sometimes	announcer	slide	team)	

Word Checkout
1. False   2. True   3. False   4. True   5. False

Words "To Go"
out in left field = you don't know what's happening = you are confused
batting a thousand = you are doing everything exactly right = you are not making mistakes

The Card Shop   This is a card for someone you want to see or talk to soon.
To touch base = to visit or talk with

LESSON 12   Too Many, Too Much
This lesson is about making choices in the supermarket. It can be very difficult. What can you do?

Word Basket: Target Words
confusing   way

Reading 1

delicious	which	situation	for now	grocery store
tuna	upset	hungry	fast	wrong
salad	can't	idea	canned	
needs	going crazy	try	story	
can	deal with	again	supermarket	

Reading 2

note	believe	left	triple	funny
Mom	kinds	nothing	cheeseburger	sad
told	couldn't	just	fries	contains
eat right	decision	fast food place	shake	
watch your	stood	rest	irregular	
cholesterol	finally	pet peeve	hate	

Word Checkout
1. confused/upset   2. nothing   3. triple cheeseburger, fries, and a shake   4. Mom (mother)

Words "To Go"
Shop 'til you drop. = Go shopping until you are very, very tired. = Shop for a very long time.
Decisions, decisions! = It is difficult to make choices.

The Card Shop   You can send a card like this one when you have forgotten to write or call for a long time. It says that you're sorry.

LESSON 13   Loss
This lesson is about the death of a person in someone's family. What do you do? What can you say?

Word Basket: Target Words

loss	comfortable	continue	funeral	
	death	conversation	customs	

Reading 1

arrived	past tense	stockings	hand	clothes
seats	shouted	sweater	quietly	
take out	yelled	silent	acting	
assignments	wearing	put up	moment	

Reading 2

began	how old was (he/	I'm so sorry	tears
what's the matter	she)	ago	peacefully
died	heart attack	in his sleep	

Word Checkout
1. False   2. False   3. True   4. True   5. True

Words "To Go"
He/she passed away. = He/she died.
We're thinking of you. = We're sorry about the death in your family.

The Card Shop   The cards you send to the family when a person dies are called "sympathy" cards. *Sympathy* means knowing how another person feels, especially when they have had a loss or are sad. A sympathy card should be sent **only** when someone has died, to tell the family you feel sorry about the death.

Lesson 14   Love
This lesson is about romantic love. How do people fall in love? What do they do? What do they say?

Word Basket: Target Words
love

Reading 1

lucky	hell	(worked) hard	so far	middle-aged
unlucky	young	nothing to do	*the* person	luck
heaven	old	with	being/falling in	half-true
over	destiny	met	love	explain

Reading 2

sweethearts	thought	soon after	together
smart	unhappy	discovered	more than
handsome	lives	decided	

Word Checkout
1. False   2. True   3. False   4. False   5. True

Words "To Go"
Love makes the world go round. = Love makes everything happy and easy. =
   Love is the energy that makes things happen.
All's fair in love and war. = Anything you do to win love or to fight a war is OK.

The Card Shop   This card is for Valentine's Day, February 14. It is an old poem. It is for someone you love.

LESSON 15   Life
This lesson is about the birth of a baby. This birth brings joy to everyone.

Word Basket: Target Words
life   baby

Reading 1

arrival	lbs. (See also	how long	parents
clinic	Word Store)	in. (See also	born
how much	oz. (See also	Word Store)	weigh
	Word Store)	proud	

Reading 2

special	common	healthy	for years	length
delivery	average	grandparents	whole	birthday
midnight	normal	even longer	thrilled	time of day
in the wee hours	didn't care if	hoping	welcome	

Word Checkout
Robert Rico; On Tuesday, November 8, at 4:30 P.M.; At the Downtown Hospital; 8 lbs. 7 oz.; 20 in.; Rita and Raymond Rico

Words "To Go"
bundle of joy = new baby
the pitter patter of little feet = the sound of a little child walking

The Card Shop   This card should be sent to the parents of a new baby. It is also nice to include older brothers and sisters in your congratulations.

The English Alphabet

Capital letters:

A B C D E F G H I J K L M N O P Q R S T U V W X Y Z

Small letters:

a b c d e f g h i j k l m n o p q r s t u v w x y z

Days of the Week
Sunday
Monday
Tuesday
Wednesday
Thursday
Friday
Saturday

Months of the Year
January   July
February   August
March   September
April   October
May   November
June   December

Seasons of the Year
spring
summer
fall (autumn)
winter

Colors
black
white
grey
brown
yellow
red
blue
green
purple
orange
pink
olive
violet

Numbers
0	zero	11	eleven	21	twenty-one	100 one hundred
1	one	12	twelve	22	twenty-two	101 one hundred and one
2	two	13	thirteen	23	twenty-three	200 two hundred
3	three	14	fourteen	24	twenty-four	1000 one thousand
4	four	15	fifteen	25	twenty-five	10,000 ten thousand
5	five	16	sixteen	26	twenty-six	100,000 one hundred thousand
6	six	17	seventeen	27	twenty-seven	
7	seven	18	eighteen	28	twenty-eight	1,000,000 one million
8	eight	19	nineteen	29	twenty-nine	1,000,000,000 one billion
9	nine	20	twenty	30	thirty	1,000,000,000,000 one trillion
10	ten			40	forty	
				50	fifty	
				60	sixty	
				70	seventy	
				80	eighty	
				90	ninety	

Languages of the World (other than English)

Aboriginal
Afrikaans
Albanian
Alsatian German
Altaic
Amharic
Arabic
Armenian
Aymara
Bahasa Indonesian
Bambara
Bantu
Basque
Bengali
Berber
Breton
Bulgarian
Byeloruss
Canton Dialect
Catalan
Caucasian
Chechuto
Chichewa
Creole
Crioulo
Czech
Danish
Dari Persian
Divehi
Djerma

Dutch
Dzongka Tibetan
Fang
Farsi
Finnish
Flemish
French/African Patois
French Patois
Frisian
Fukien
Galician
Galla
German
Gilbertese
Gollato
Guarani
Hakka Dialect
Hassaniya Arabic
Hausa
Hebrew
Hindi
Hmong
Hungarian
Ibo
Icelandic
Indian
Indo-European
Irish Gaelic
Jamaican Creole
Japanese

Javanese
Khaikha Mongolian
Khmer
Kinyarwandu
Kirundi
Korean
Krio
Kurdish
Kurkish
Kyongsangto
Lao
Lapp
Latin
Latvian
Lesotho
Lithuanian
Luganda
Luxembourgish
Macedonian
Malagasy Dialect
Malay
Maltese
Mandarin
Chinese
Maori
Maya-Quiche Dialect
Melanesian
Melanesian Pidgin

Merina
Monagesque
More
Nahuatl
Namkyongto
Nauraun
Ndebele
Nepali
Newari
Niger-Congo
Norwegian
Papuan
Patois
Persian
Pidgin English
Pilipino
Police Motu
Polish
Pushtu
Pyonganto
Quechua
Quenchua Dialect
Romanian
Romansch
Russian
Samoan
Sangho
Seoul
Serbo-Croatian
Setswana

Shanghai Dialect
Shona
Shungchondo
Sinhala
Siswati
Slovak
Somali
Sranan Tongo
Sudani Tribal
Swahili
Swedish
Taiwan
Tamil
Thai
Tibetan
Tigre
Tongan
Turkish
Tuvaluan
Ukranian
Uralian
Urdu
Uzbek
Valencian
Vietnamese
Vigus
Welsh
West Asian
Yiddish
Yoruba